D0367628

The Amish Detective Amish Vengeance

Hannah Schrock

Table of Contents

Liv turned off the car's engine and stepped out into the chilly air. It wasn't that cold, really—spring was on its way—but she shivered nonetheless. Even the heavy jacket, with its fur-lined hood, couldn't keep her warm. Nothing could anymore.

She looked around the landscape, doing a full three hundred-sixty-degree turn. It was flat. There wasn't much to redeem it at that time of year. She knew that once spring and summer came, the land would be green and lush, filled with cornstalks and whatever crops the farmers grew. On a gray, cool day such as the one on which she visited her best friend's childhood home, it looked desolate. As hopeless and desolate as her broken heart.

Rebecca. She flashed in front of Liv's eyes, blocking out the expanse of barren land. She usually came when Liv closed her eyes at night, but with so much of her in the air and in Liv's head, she showed herself in the middle of the day. Her Rebecca. The girl who once made Liv laugh so hard that she cried. Her best friend, her partner in crime. In a pool of blood on the bedroom floor.

Liv shook her head to clear away the image. A tear had escaped her eye, and she brushed a quick hand over it. She was used to crying. Sometimes she thought there were no tears left in her. How could a person possibly cry so much? Then, she would start again. And again. At the most random times, too.

She shivered again, sliding her hands into her pockets and walking in place to get her blood moving. She looked to her left, toward the cluster of farms where Rebecca grew up. Until she died, Liv had no idea of her best friend's past. There she was, thinking they told each other everything, when Rebecca had hidden a somewhat enormous secret from her for years.

Liv got back into the car, pointing in the direction of the farms around a mile down the road.

The closer she got, the heavier Rebecca's presence felt. All around her. She could hardly breathe. She saw her best friend again—on her back, head turned to the side. Eyes wide open, staring blankly as Liv opened the bedroom door. A pool of nearly black blood had spread beneath her, congealed by the time Liv found her. She stared, seemingly straight into Liv's eyes. Demanding she make things right by bringing the killer to justice.

It's all in my imagination, Liv thought. She wasn't looking at me. She was already gone.

She shook herself to clear the morbid thought away, then pulled into the parking lot of a small store. hers was the only car at the end of a row of buggies. She sat there for a long time, wondering if visiting Amish country was such a good idea. Looking out the window to the buggies, she had to laugh at herself. How much more could she have stuck out? Talk about a sore thumb.

She leaned her weary head back against the seat and closed her eyes. Now that she had parked, exhaustion overtook her. Sleep had been a fleeting, almost nonexistent state. Every time she closed her eyes in the dark, Rebecca was there. Those eyes. Staring. Demanding.

Liv remembered the night she found her. It might as well have been a day, a minute, instead of weeks.

It was a typically long day at the office, full of deadlines and last-minute emergencies. She hadn't even had time to eat lunch. By the time she'd left it was dark outside, and she was hangry—angry because she was hungry. All she could do was look forward to the promise of home. A cozy apartment, takeout, maybe a glass or two of wine to unwind after the struggle to hit a deadline. She'd hit it, but such fast-paced work always took it out of her.

She took a cab home instead of walking, since the neighborhood wasn't exactly Mayberry once darkness fell. It was cold, too, her breath hanging in a fog around her head when she stepped out of the cab and dashed up to the front door of the apartment building. She'd wondered if she could talk Rebecca into ordering Chinese with her as she jogged up the narrow stairs to their third-floor apartment.

When she'd opened the door to the living room, the first thing she'd heard was the TV. Rebecca had it tuned to some ridiculous talk show—the sort of thing she never watched. The audience was screaming over what a guest said, and Liv turned to volume down. "Beck?" she called out. Her bedroom door was closed—Liv assumed she went inside to change or something, and left the TV going.

She didn't answer. Liv idly flipped through mail, waiting for her to come out. After several minutes and another attempt to get her attention, she'd put down the magazine she'd been looking at. A seed of fear took root in her stomach.

"Rebecca? Are you all right?" Liv had knocked on the bedroom door. No answer. She'd pressed her ear against it. No sound. "Beck? Are you sick?"

Her hand had closed over the knob, and she'd quickly pushed the door open. Almost like ripping off a Band-Aid—all at once. She was afraid Rebecca had hurt herself somehow.

Nothing could have prepared Liv for what she'd found. It took a split second for her to register the sight of her roommate's dead body. When the neighbors came running, she was still screaming incoherently.

Liv opened her eyes, looking around. When had she dozed off? The line of buggies was smaller—time had passed. So tired. She wondered whether it had been a smart idea to do all that driving when she was so sleepy, but it was already done.

She shook her head, scrubbing shaky hands over her face to get the blood flowing. Rolling down the car window and taking a deep breath of the cool air helped clear her head—though the fresh, pungent aroma of horse manure wasn't exactly pleasant.

There was no way she could live with that image in her head for the rest of her life. It would drive her crazy. She would finally spend enough sleepless nights to the point where she would lose her mind. Or she would fall asleep behind the wheel, as she very well could have while making the drive from the city out to Amish country. She pushed back her long, cocoa colored hair. When was the last time she did more than wash it and put it in a ponytail? And even then, sometimes she didn't bother to wash it. There had been days immediately following the murder when Liv couldn't get out of bed. But she never slept for more than a few minutes at a time. She would stare at the ceiling, watching the shadows change as morning turned to night, then back to morning. She saw Rebecca's face in front of her every time she closed her eyes. She couldn't close her eyes.

She looked around again, wondering if coffee was something the people in that neck of the woods ever heard of. She got out of the car, zipping the jacket to her throat, and walked down the paved sidewalk. The store she'd parked in front of looked busy enough, though Liv got the impression it was strictly an Amish store. Meanwhile, other stores up and down the street appeared to cater to the outsiders, like her. Souvenir shops. Tourist traps, more like. She marveled at how many people walked in and out. Wanting a little piece of the Amish lifestyle for themselves, without making the commitment.

A coffee shop. She sighed with relief, then walked inside. Starbucks, it was not, but it would do. She ordered a latte and looked around while she waited. Everyone there was like her. Well, maybe not just like her. She got a very touristy vibe from them. She wasn't there for fun.

She didn't take a seat, choosing to drink the coffee as she walked, instead. Checking the address on her phone, she looked at the map. It was only a mile to her destination.

It was time she started getting answers in her friend's death. She had no choice but to start from square one.

Liv met Rebecca when she was twenty years old, at a college party. She had only gone in the first place to get the attention of a guy she had a crush on—when it became clear that he was more interested in another girl, she'd sulked in the corner for a little while, nursing a drink. He had invited her, darn it, with the promise that they'd spend time together.

"You look like you're having about as much fun as I am." Liv had turned to find a pretty young girl standing next to her.

"Gee, was it that obvious?" she asked, grinning.

"Who is he?" The stranger scanned the room.

"Who is who?"

"The boy you like, who isn't paying attention to you."

Liv gasped. She was very blunt, wasn't she? She didn't know her. A stranger who didn't know what she felt.

"You're wrong," Liv said, smiling. "It's not like that at all."

"No? Then why were you shooting death looks at the tall, lanky guy in the opposite corner before I spoke to you?" The over-friendly, blunt girl smirking knowingly, swinging her long, blonde hair over one shoulder.

Liv sized her up. She wasn't trying to be nasty. If anything, it seemed like she had a sad sort of understanding. Like she had been there before and knew her pain. Liv opened her mouth to reply, but nothing came out.

"Come on," the strange girl said, taking Liv's cup and putting it on the closest flat surface. "Let's get out of here. We'll get something to eat, and you can tell me all about it."

"I'm not hungry," Liv said, even as she put on my coat.

"I am. I'll buy you a cup of coffee. Come on. I could use the company, and this party is lame." The small, blonde girl led the way, just like she always would. She was petite and soft-spoken, but with a strong personality.

"Trust me," she said, walking beside Liv down the wide main street, just off-campus, "I know how it feels."

"How what feels?" Liv asked.

"Getting dumped. Or, rather, being unhappy because you can't be with the person you want."

"You know how that goes, huh?" She looked roughly twelve years old, with her super clear skin and bright eyes.

"I do. I think girls like us should stick together and help each other. Buck each other up when we're down. Somebody did it for me, once, when I needed it. I'm paying it forward with you." She walked into the diner just down the street from the party, and Liv followed her.

"Thanks…"

"Rebecca." She grinned. "Rebecca Blough."

"Liv Roberts."

Just like that, they were best friends.

Liv thought she knew everything about her. Being roommates with a person for nearly five years, you learn about them. Likes, dislikes. Idiosyncrasies. Her penchant for 80s music. Her love of Taco Bell. Her inability to get through sappy romantic movies without crying.

The off-key way she sang in the shower, belting out show tunes— another obsession, one which sometimes woke Liv from a sound sleep. The way she never put a new bag in the can after emptying the trash. The way she tended to misplace bills when they came in, leaving them unpaid until the electric company threatened to shut off their service.

When caught in one of those more irritating habits, Rebecca would flash a charming smile and all would be forgotten…until the next time she did the next thing to drive Liv crazy.

She knew so many things about her best friend—all except for the fact that Rebecca had been born and raised Amish.

"Are you sure?" Liv watched the detective pace her living room, a mug of hot tea held between her trembling hands. The downstairs neighbor wrapped a blanket around her shoulders. Rebecca's body had been taken away, but the cops stayed behind to collect evidence and ask questions.

"We are, miss. Her name and birthdate were run through the system as soon as we checked her license. She attended college with you, right?"

"Yes."

"When she first applied, she listed her home address as one in Lancaster. There is no phone number attached to that address. My team tells me it's a home in the middle of Amish country, part of a fairly strict order."

Her head buzzed. First Rebecca's murder, then finding out she'd hidden such a huge part of her life.

"Did she ever talk about her family?" the detective asked.

She opened her mouth, sure she could think of at least one instance in which Rebecca had spoken of them with anything other than thinly-veiled contempt. Only she couldn't come up with anything. Not a single example.

"That doesn't make any sense," she protested. "Beck told me everything."

"But she never talked about a family."

"She never wanted to. I guessed she came from a bad family You know? Abuse, maybe. When we first met, I asked her about them. She told me she had no relationship with them. I figured, it's her life. She seemed happy enough with them. It didn't seem to bother her at all."

Only it did seem to bother her. She might not have come right out and told Liv she missed having a family, but she showed it in a million little ways. She always got a little depressed around the holidays, no matter how hard she tried to hide it. She was the most cheerful person Liv knew, and she could decorate a tree like nobody's business. Only sometimes, every so often, Liv would glance in her direction and see her frowning. Sometimes her chin would even tremble. Or, Liv would find her standing by the window, looking out at the snow with a sort of wistful expression on her face. She might have been cheerful on the outside, but there was a deep core of sadness inside her. One she never let her best friend anywhere near.

The more Liv thought it over in the days and weeks after the discovery, the more it made sense. Rebecca seemed to have no past. Even if she didn't specifically talk about her family, it stood to reason that she would have memories of other times. The sorts of things all kids knew about. The ice cream truck pulling around the corner in the summer. Carnivals. Her first roller coaster. Her first dance. Something. She never spoke of those times in any way. When Liv did, she'd find a way to change the subject.

Liv shook her head when she thought about it, as she always did. Why hadn't she seen it at the time? Why hadn't she pressed Rebecca to be upfront about it? She didn't know what it all meant, but it led her to believe there was a lot about Rebecca which she didn't know—and it was that secret side of her that got her killed.

She couldn't prove it, of course. Not yet. But she would. If it was there, she would prove it, somehow.

Otherwise, the police were just as hopeless as she was. The girl had no enemies. She was the sweetest, most thoughtful friend a person could have. She had taught at a special needs school, and was universally adored. Patient, loving, supportive, energetic. She had plenty of friends and one or two special boyfriends, but nothing ever came of those relationships. Still, she always stayed friends with the men in question.

They had been interrogated, too, all of them. They all had rock-solid alibis, and all were visibly crushed when they found out Rebecca was dead—and how she died. They had nothing but good things to say about her.

It wasn't even a robbery. There was no attempted assault. Nothing except five blows with an object similar to a large craving knife.

"Murderers aren't always strangers," the detective told Liv. They sat together at the police station as she gave him yet another statement.

She shook her head, rubbing her hands over her arms. She felt so cold, and the dank atmosphere of the station didn't help. "I'm telling you. I've known her for five years, and she didn't have a single enemy. Maybe it was mistaken identity or something."

"Do you have any enemies?"

Liv gasped—she hadn't considered that the killer might have confused them and killed the wrong girl. "Not that I'm aware of."

"Mmm-hmm. What is it you do, Miss Roberts?"

"You can call me Liv. I'm a reporter for the Inquirer."

"Aren't you the big expose writer? Didn't you contribute to the series on corruption in City Hall?"

She smirked. "If you knew who I am and what I do, why did you ask?"

He grinned. "You got me. I ask that to point out that maybe you were the one with enemies. You might have rubbed somebody the wrong way."

Tears flooded her eyes. "Don't do that to me. Don't make me responsible for this."

"You're not responsible, no matter what. Even if you did make an enemy, they were the one who did this. Not you. You didn't make it happen."

"But you're saying my actions might have led to it, even indirectly." She burst into tears, holding her face in her hands. Her body shook with sobs.

He waited until the storm of emotion passed, then said, "I think it would be best to review anyone who might have a grudge against you."

They went through a list of names—it was a short list. She hadn't had a long career yet. The police followed up on a few leads, but came up with nothing. There were no fingerprints anywhere in the apartment, no footprints. Not even a stray hair. Absolutely nothing.

The detective called her one day, beyond frustrated. "Either the person who did this is a ghost, or they're the most skillful hit man I've ever seen."

At that point, the idea of a hit man came into play. Still, the theory never made sense, and the cops never found any evidence to support the theory except for a lack of evidence pointing anywhere else. That was no way to build a case.

That was when Liv decided to take matters into her own hands, requesting a few days away from work and driving the two hours to Lancaster. It was time to talk to Rebecca's family—if they didn't slam the door in her face, that was. She had no idea why Rebecca left the community, under what circumstances. It could have been something terrible—judging from the way she never spoke of her family, Liv thought it might be.

She couldn't go home without trying, though, and she gave

herself a pep talk while driving the last mile to the house in question. It's all worth it. She's worth it. Don't be scared. You're only asking questions. They can't get upset for that.

They could, though. That was the worst part—not knowing how they'd treat her. She'd never known an Amish person before, had never interacted with one.

Yes, I have. Rebecca, of course. Liv prayed her family was as kind and understanding as Rebecca had been.

It was a small, quaint little house. There was a large barn behind it, what she thought might be a chicken coop, and acres of land. Nothing was growing, but she guessed it would be quite lush and fruitful when summer came.

Was this where Rebecca grew up? Did she swing on the tire attached by a rope to the tree? Did she feed the chickens and collect eggs? Why did she leave?

What followed her?

Liv parked at the end of the dirt path leading to the house—she didn't want to drive right up, afraid of startling the inhabitants. She saw two young girls approaching in what she knew were Amish clothes—plain dresses, black aprons. White caps on their heads, with white ribbons hanging behind them. They wore what looked like homemade cardigans over their dresses, and thick black stockings.

"Excuse me?" Liv waved to them, smiling. They froze like deer in headlights. "Can you tell me where Joshua Blough lives?"

They looked at each other, then at her. She wondered if they spoke English.

"Can you help me, please?" She looked from one to the other. Their eyes were wide. One of them finally pointed, wordlessly, to the house at the end of the path. Then, they hurried off like Liv was on fire and they were afraid to burn.

She was an outsider, she realized. They were afraid of her. No doubt they had heard all sorts of stories about people like her. The ones who wore jeans and drove cars.

She turned toward the house and began the walk down the path. The house looked empty—funny, she thought, how people from the "outside" tended to look to the sidewalk or driveway to see if a person was home. There was no way for her to know.

She climbed the stairs, knees shaking. Now that she was there, she had no choice but to keep going, but anxiety threatened to overwhelm her. Sweaty palms, a racing heart. Her hand shook as she raised it, clenching it into a fist.

She knocked on the door.

When the young man with the very blue eyes opened the door, Liv knew what it felt like to be punched in the stomach. All the air left her body in a big rush.

"Are you all right?" he asked. She marveled over the fact that he didn't even know her, but he asked if she was all right. How totally the opposite of what a person from her world would do. If a stranger showed up at her door and acted like they just saw a ghost, she thought she would have bolted the door and call the police.

She steadied herself against the doorframe, taking a few deep breaths. The cool air revived her. "I'm okay," she breathed, her voice a shaky whisper. "I'm sorry to disturb you."

"Not at all. Please. Do you need a chair?" He motioned inside the house. "I can fetch you a glass of water."

She looked into his blue eyes, and tears filled her own. He was so like his sister. Rebecca would have done the same thing for anyone in need. Like that first night, when she rescued Liv from the party.

"I feel as though I should introduce myself, first," she said, slowly. Fighting back the sobs growing in her throat. "My name is Liv Roberts. I was the roommate of Rebecca Blough."

He looked as though she'd hit him—probably the same way she looked moments earlier, when she saw a male version of Rebecca's face staring at her. His brow furrowed, as though he was in pain.

"My sister," he whispered. Of course, she was. They could have been twins, practically.

"I'm so sorry. I'm sorry if this brings you any pain."

"Please, you must come in. If you knew my Rebecca, I need to speak with you." My Rebecca. Liv's ears didn't miss the endearment. He loved his sister. She breathed a sigh of relief at not being kicked off the porch and the land.

"My name is Joshua," he said, extending a hand. Liv took it in hers. Strong, calloused. A man who worked hard. "Have a seat. I insist on getting you something to drink. I have so many questions for you." He disappeared into the kitchen. It was she who had questions for him, but maybe they could take turns.

Liv looked around the living room. It was lovely—simple, but lovely. She wondered where the woman of the house was. What would she think of her husband spending time alone with a stranger?

"Here you are." He brought out a tray with what looked like iced tea in tall glasses, and a plate of cookies.

"Are those sugar cookies?" she asked, smiling.

"Yes. My Mamm makes them and brings them to me. They were always our favorite—Rebecca's and mine."

Liv smiled. "She used to make them. At Christmas." She leaned forward, taking one. The first bite brought back so many memories, she thought their weight would crush her. She closed her eyes.

When she opened them, she looked at him. He smiled, but it was a smile of great sadness. His eyes, Rebecca's eyes, were so sad, too. And tired. She noticed for the first time the dark circles under them, the paleness of his skin.

"I'm sorry to bother you," she said again. "Showing up like this. Only…there was no other way for me to contact you."

"Of course," he agreed, with a kind grin. "That's to be expected."

"So, you knew of Rebecca's passing?"

He nodded, the grin disappearing from his face. "Yes. The police came out to tell me."

"I'm sure it was a great shock to you."

He nodded again. "We had not been in contact for many years, you see. Many years. I didn't know anything about her life. I only knew she moved to the city when she left."

"How long ago was that?"

"She didn't tell you?"

She shook her head, wanting to put it delicately. "She didn't tell me anything about her life. I'm sorry."

He shrugged. "I'm not surprised. I don't take it personally."

"You don't?"

"No. I knew how unhappy she was, and with good reason. I couldn't hold it against her. I've prayed so much for her over the years, hoping she finally found peace in her new life."

"Was she…troubled?" She turned toward him on the sofa. He sat hunched forward, elbows on his knees, his head slightly downturned.

"I wouldn't say that. She had troubling things in her life. As did I, honestly."

"Can I ask? I'm sorry, I don't mean to pry…"

"You're not prying." Again with that kind smile. "You want to know about her old life, and I want to know about her new life. We can help one another."

She couldn't help but smile back. "I feel the same way."

He leaned further forward, taking a cookie, then picking up the glass of iced tea. After he swallowed half the glass, his face turned thoughtful. He was deciding where to begin.

"Our childhood was not an easy one," he began. "Our Daed did not abide by the Amish way of life."

"I'm sorry. Daed, did you say?"

She thought she saw a blush color his cheeks, above a blonde beard. "Sorry. Our father."

"Oh, I see." She thought she should have figured that out herself.

"Daed had a good heart, I'm sure. At one time. However, he began drinking at an early age. Now, you must understand, imbibing is strictly against the rules of the Ordung."

"I'm sure." What the heck was an Ordung? Again, she needed to use the context clues. Their order, maybe?

"He was also unfaithful."

"Oh, I see." It was her turn to blush. She had no idea, when she arrived, that she would be uncovering so many gloomy family secrets.

"The worst part was, he didn't try to cover up his deeds. No matter where Rebecca or I went, we heard the whispers. The jeers. Our father had affairs with many women. Englischers."

"Outsiders?"

"Yes, that is our word for those not of our faith."

"I see." Liv wished she'd started taking notes when they first began speaking. So many new words to keep track of. "So I'm an Englischer?"

"Right. So, Daed did his deeds. Mamm was not the sort of woman to ever put up a fight. She was meek, afraid of him. She wouldn't raise her voice to the cat, much less her husband. I don't know how he terrorized her while Rebecca and I weren't around. I only know she was afraid of him."

"Oh, how terrible. I'm so sorry." To think, Englischers had an idea about the Amish, that they were perfect. It turned out they were only human, just like anybody else.

"It's not easy, growing up that way. When people laugh at you, it was especially difficult because our family shame was viewed as weakness, evil. The adults reasoned that if Rebecca and I were raised by such a weak, evil man, how could we follow Gott as we should? The sins of the father, as they say."

"So you were…outcast?"

"In a way. We weren't allowed to play with most of the children. We had each other, though. We were very close as a result.

Sometimes it felt like we were all we had. Mamm was often too ill to be relied on."

"She was sickly?"

"Yes. There were times when I thought it was a broken heart, silly as it sounds. When I was younger. She was always sad, fretful, flinching when Daed came home from a night at the pub. Her illness always seemed to grow poorer when he was at his worst."

Liv thought it no wonder Rebecca told her nothing about her childhood. She wanted to forget about it—who wouldn't? She ran away. It couldn't have been easy, but Liv couldn't blame her for it.

"Was that why she left, then? Because of the shame?"

"No, not directly. The shame led to the reason. The thing which made it all unbearable. You see, Rebecca was in love with a boy from our community. His name was Adam. He loved her, too. They wanted to get married."

Liv had a sinking feeling in her chest. "Let me guess. She wasn't good enough."

"According to Adam's father. Exactly. He didn't want his son marrying the daughter of a man like our Daed. So, that was that."

"They couldn't get married, just because his father wouldn't allow it?"

"It's very important in our community that we follow Gott's law, which means obeying our parents' wishes. Besides, if he married Rebecca, it wouldn't be just his family who shunned him. It could have been the entire Ordung, the whole community. Community is all we have, you see. We support each other, we rely on each other. Their lives would have been destroyed."

"I see. So the relationship ended."

"And so did Rebecca's life in the community. She left. I never saw her again."

Her head spun, and she leaned against the back of the sofa to collect herself. "How old was she?"

"Eighteen."

For six years, Rebecca had been gone. He never saw her. It must have been terrible for him.

"Do your parents ever talk about her?"

"My parents are deceased."

"Jeez. I keep stepping in it."

"It?"

"Uh, uncomfortable stuff. Horse manure."

He chuckled. "Got it. Yes, Daed died not long after Rebecca left. He was hit by a car, stumbling home one night after drinking. He walked out into the road, the car struck him. He died immediately."

"I'm sorry."

"I'm not." Her eyes widened at the coldness of Joshua's words. From such a sweet-looking man, with such a sweet, quiet nature, it was shocking to hear something so callous. "He brought it on himself. He caused my family nothing but pain. My mother died not long after that. I had thought that maybe, she would finally be happy. She could live life without him. I was wrong. She was too far gone by then. Too sick. I couldn't even contact Rebecca to tell her, since I didn't know where she was."

There was so much sadness in his voice, but he tried to mask it with anger. And it was righteous anger. Liv couldn't deny him the right to it. She would have been angry, too, if her entire life were tainted by the actions of her parents.

The sadness was there, though, whether he hid it or not. Just like Rebecca's sadness, which she couldn't hide. They had more in common than their looks.

Liv guessed he had felt very alone at that time, and maybe a little hurt that Rebecca left just when everything really fell apart. Maybe he could have used her in his life when his parents both died. It couldn't have been easy to handle alone.

"I'm very sorry you faced these things," she said. "I know Rebecca would have come home if she knew."

"How do you know that?" he asked. His voice was flat; like he didn't believe her.

"I knew her." She shrugged. "I knew who she was. I knew her heart. There were so many times when I sensed a real longing for something—I didn't know what, since she never told me anything about her past. I only knew that it had to be from her past, if that makes any sense."

"She probably longed for him. Adam. It's like as not she never got over him."

She didn't want to tell Joshua that his sister had done her best to get over her first love, dating a fairly decent number of boys over five years. She discreetly sidestepped the remark with a noncommittal, "That may be."

Liv looked around again, taking a long sip of the iced tea, eating another cookie. Just like the ones Rebecca used to make, singing Christmas carols all the while. Liv missed her so much. "You have a lovely home," she said, wanting to clear the tension in the air, if only for a minute.

"Thank you," he smiled graciously.

"Was this your childhood home?"

"It was. I lived here with my wife, as well." His voice caught in his throat. Past tense. Oh, no. She didn't have to ask. She wasn't sure she wanted to hear the pain when he answered.

This poor man, she thought. He looked young, healthy. And so very heartsick.

"Tell me about her," he asked, leaning toward her. For the first time in the hour since she'd arrived, she saw a spark in his eye. She had to oblige him—besides, she wanted to talk about Rebecca.

"She was my best friend," Liv said, grinning. "For five years, we shared our apartment. We went to the same school."

"She went to school?" he asked.

"Is that unusual?"

"For us, yes. We only go up to the eighth grade."

"Hmm. She graduated college. Maybe she took the test for a GED —um, to make up for not attending high school."

"I see. I guess that's what she did. She was a very determined girl."

Liv rolled her eyes. "That's one word to describe her! Stubborn would be another one."

He laughed with her. "Yes, that was my sister. A mule." They laughed together. He had a nice laugh—rich, warm. He didn't do enough laughing, Liv thought. He needed to do more of it. He was a young man.

"She was a teacher. She specialized in helping children with special needs. The ones who didn't learn as easily, or who needed a little extra attention."

"She had a kind heart, didn't she?"

"She did. The kindest I knew. Her students loved her, their parents loved her. She helped even the ones they considered beyond help. The ones too far gone. She brought them around, helped them smile and laugh and have confidence in themselves. It was inspiring." Liv looked him in the eye. "In a way, she lives on in them. Does that sound silly?"

"Not at all. It's a relief, really. A comfort. She did good work. She might not have put Gott first, the way we were taught, but she did His work."

It was different, hearing a person talk about God so freely and openly, the way he did. Refreshing. Liv wondered what it would be like to live such a God-centric life.

"What else can you tell me about her?" he asked, more eager than before.

She thought about it. She didn't want to tell him anything that might be considered unsavory. What did the Amish consider distasteful? "She had a lot of friends. She always laughed."

"She was funny, too, wasn't she?"

"Extremely. One time she made me laugh so hard, I…well," she blushed. "I laughed pretty hard. Let's just leave it at that." He blushed and didn't reply, but she sensed he understood what she was trying to say. Liv laughed self-consciously.

"Was she doing well, there? In the Englischer world? Was she happy?"

She could be completely honest about that. "Yes. She was happy. She made a good life for herself. A job, friends, a nice apartment. In our world, that's pretty good for a twenty-four-year old. There was no reason she couldn't have had a brilliant future. I always thought she would make an ideal mother. She took care of me for as long as I knew her, and she was a year younger than me. I should have been the one taking care of her." She told him the story of the night Rebecca found her at the party—and as she told it, she realized Rebecca had been talking about Adam when she talked about getting hurt by a boy. Poor Rebecca.

"You say she had a lot of friends," he mused.

"Oh, so many. I threw her a birthday party when she turned twenty-one. I don't think our apartment ever had so many people in it, honestly. She knew every person there, too, and took time with each of them. It was her party, but she treated everyone else like they were the important ones."

"She was a very selfless person," he mused.

"I'm sorry you couldn't have been there to see it."

"I would rather she was here," he admitted. "I don't think I would do well in the Englischer world. I wasn't like Rebecca—she always had interest in that world. She wanted to know why she couldn't go to school the way Englischer girls did." Liv guessed that was why education was so important to her. That was all she could do anymore, though. Guess. She could never ask her best friend anything, ever again.

"I'm glad you came," he said, smiling with obvious relief. "You don't know what it was like, hearing Rebecca died. Not having any idea what her life was like, who she knew, why this happened."

"We still don't know why," Liv reminded him. "We might never know why."

He looked at his hands. She noticed he wore a wedding band. How long had his wife been gone? He had been through so much. He cleared his throat. "Do you know why? Do you have any idea?"

She drew a deep, shaky breath and shook her head. "I wish I did. That's part of the reason why I came here—I wanted to know more about her, to maybe piece something together. Right now, there's nothing."

He sighed unhappily. "I'm sorry to hear that."

"I'm sorry to say it. I hate thinking that the person who did this is walking around, free. Living their life, while the best person I ever knew isn't living hers anymore." Her chin trembled, and she looked away. The mantel above the fireplace held a few candles. That was one thing that threw her about the house: No family photos. Had she ever been in a house without family photos? Then again, she wondered if Joshua would put up photos even if he had them, judging from his pitiful childhood.

Still, he had his faith. That impressed Liv. When he spoke of God, it was with great reverence. If she were him, her heart might have been hardened beyond redemption. She saw where Rebecca got her endless kindness. How she could forgive, so easily. She might have left her home, but the tenets of her faith clung to her.

"What is it you do for a living, Liv?" He chuckled at the way the sentence came out, and Liv had to join him when she heard his laughter. He sounded younger, better when he chuckled like that.

"I'm a reporter."

"For a newspaper?"

"That's right."

He looked interested. "What do you write about?"

"It's not very important—hardly worth talking about," she said, feeling silly. Everything she did and said felt silly, when compared to Joshua's seriousness.

"What is it?"

She rolled her eyes, grinning. "I write about new restaurants, bars, that sort of thing. I go there and taste the food, and report about it. When a restaurant closes, I write about it. Food trends— the ingredients chefs are using. That sort of thing."

He frowned for the briefest moment. "That is interesting. Why would you say it isn't?"

She shrugged. "It doesn't seem very important. Compared to what you do."

"I'm a farmer."

"That's not what I mean." Liv couldn't explain it, and her tongue tied when she tried. She blushed when she realized that compared to him, her life felt very trivial. They felt silent— extremely silent, in fact. Liv never noticed how much low noise was always present in her life. Computer fans, the fridge, traffic sounds. It was almost eerie, sitting in such perfect quiet.

"I want to know what happened to her." He raised his eyes to meet hers, and there was a grim determination in them.

"So do I. I think I'll need your help, though."

"And I'm sure I'll need yours. You can navigate the Englischer world much better than I can. Without you, I wouldn't have known anything about the last six years of her life." He sighed. "Even if we never find anything else, thank you for giving me that much."

"I'm glad I could do that for you," she whispered. "If I were you, I would want to know. I don't know how you could have gone so long without any information about her."

"It wasn't easy. I think Gott sent you to me." Liv blushed at his kind words.

He knew it wasn't right, spending so much time with an Englischer. At first, he'd allowed her inside the home because she looked so stricken at the sight of him. It was clear moments later why she had that reaction—she saw the resemblance to Rebecca. Strangers used to assume they were twins, and even those who knew them best had sometimes commented on the resemblance. When Liv rocked back on her heels in surprise, he had to take her in.

That wasn't against the rules of the Ordung. Contact with Englischers was not strictly forbidden. It was prolonged contact which was—especially when the contact was unchaperoned, as it was while they sat together in the living room.

He couldn't help himself. She was the only connection to his sister. He would never grow tired of asking questions about her.

As they sat together, it seemed there was never an end to the conversation. He asked the pretty young Englischer every question he could think of. What did his sister like to eat? What did she do with her free time? It was gratifying to hear that she still liked to knit, just as she had from childhood.

"Mamm taught her how," he explained. "She took to it right away."

Liv smiled. "She knitted a sweater for me, once."

"She did?"

"I'll wear it the next time we see each other."

They both silent, the weight of her words hanging between them.

"I'm sorry," Liv said, shaking her head. "That was presumptuous of me."

"Not at all," he said."

"I don't want to force myself on you. I'm sure you have more than enough to do without having me hanging around."

"On the contrary." How could he tell her how lonely he was? How she was the first person he'd seen for as long as he could remember who interested him, who made him want to talk and even laugh? He couldn't. It wouldn't sound right, no matter how he said it, and it was improper. That didn't make it untrue, however.

He watched her from the corner of his eye, wanting to be discreet. She had very dark hair, he noticed, pulled up above her slim neck. She was thin, and didn't look very healthy. Over-tired, he thought. Dark circles under her eyes. Her clothing appeared to be too large for her frame. He wondered if it was due to strain after Rebecca's death, or if this Liv was merely a sickly person. He didn't know any Englischers personally, but he guessed he would look and feel much the same if his life was always noisy, busy, and completely lacking a relationship with Gott.

That was the one thing he could never understand. She might have needed to get away from their family and the stigma attached—Joshua could understand that—but how could his sister have turned her back on Gott?

"Was she religious?" he asked Liv, almost dreading the answer.

She sighed, looking at her hands. "I know what you want me to say, but I'm afraid I can't lie."

"I understand." It was a disappointment, yet he'd known what to expect.

"She was spiritual, though. I know it's not the same, but it's something. Right?" Joshua smiled at how hard Liv tried to comfort him.

"Spiritual? What's the difference?"

"I know she believed in something bigger than herself. She didn't go to church—"

"We don't have churches, either."

"You don't?" Liv's eyes widened in surprise.

"No, we meet in one another's homes. We take turns."

"Oh. That's so interesting. So there are no formal churches, then."

"Not at all."

Liv tapped her chin—Joshua had noticed her doing that earlier, signaling when she was deep in thought. "Maybe she prayed alone, then. I don't know. I do know she believed in God."

"That's good." It gave him hope. If there was one thing he knew for certain, it was that sometimes hope was all he had. Life had taught him that much.

It had been a quiet, lonely life in the little house. He kept it just as Eve had left it—nothing was out of place. Sometimes it felt as though he was waiting for her to come back. He didn't want anything to be wrong when she got back.

She would never come back. He knew it. Why couldn't he get his heart to understand it, then?

Liv leaned toward him, making Joshua remember how long it had been since he'd been so close to a woman. He pushed the thought from his mind—it was wrong, immoral—yet there was no denying how pleasant it felt. Being in the presence of a beautiful girl. She wasn't Eve, though. There was no replacing her.

"Would you mind if I did come back, then? I feel like I should go for now. It's getting late, and I'm very tired." Yes, she looked it.

"Of course I wouldn't mind." The words came out before he could stop them. His heart sank. He'd surely get his neighbors talking if they knew an Englischer made regular visits to his solitary house. There was no helping it, though. He wanted her to come back. He wanted to talk more about his sister.

He didn't want to be alone.

"I could fix you something to eat," he offered. "I'm not much of a cook, but there is stew on the stove."

"Yes, it smells good, too." She had a gentle smile. "But I'm really not very hungry. I have to try to sleep."

Try to sleep. An interesting choice of words. "You're not driving all the way back to Philadelphia tonight, are you? When you're so tired?"

"No. I have a room, not far from here. I only have to make it there." She sounded sad, tense. Exhausted.

"Can I ask you something?" In the dying light coming through the windows, he watched her face carefully. He didn't want to offend her—she might never come back, and she was his only connection to Rebecca. "Do you have trouble sleeping?"

She frowned. Her forehead creased for a moment, then it smoothed again. "Yes."

"I know how that feels."

"Everybody goes through it sometimes." She smiled, looking

down at the floor.

"I don't mean it that way. Not the normal, everyday type of sleeplessness. I went through a period of time in which it was impossible for me to sleep, after…after I lost someone I loved very much."

That got her attention. She listened more carefully, picking up her head to meet his eyes with hers. "Really? When did it stop?"

"Over time, it did. I don't know exactly how long it took. But there came a time when my need for rest outweighed what went on in my head, I suppose. I had help, too."

"What sort of help?"

"Gott. I prayed for guidance, for peace. It took time, but it did work."

She nodded thoughtfully. "I've never had much of a relationship with God. I was raised with religion, but grew out of it."

"Maybe it's time to grow back into it." He felt silly, speaking so plainly with a stranger, but she didn't seem to mind. She smiled again, in fact.

"It feels funny, saying this to you…but I feel better than I have in a long time. I don't know what it is. Maybe it's being here, where it's so quiet. You have peace, here. I can't find that at home."

He was moved by her words, but bit back the urge to say more. It would get him nowhere. He'd already learned what happened when he followed his heart. "You'll find a lot of that, here."

She noticed the way his tone changed, the subtle shift in his demeanor. It reflected on her face. She stood, taking a cue.

"I guess I should go, then. Thank you for sitting with me, for your hospitality."

"Of course." He stood, showing her to the door.

"Is the offer still good? For me to come back, I mean?"

He faced away from her, his hand on the doorknob. He knew he should take it back; tell her it wouldn't be wise to return. He knew in his heart the only option would be for them to never see each other again. There was more between them than their grief—it was unmistakable. The way they smiled at each other a bit too long, or held each other's gaze. His loneliness added to it, leaving him vulnerable. Seeing her again was a dangerous prospect.

He turned to her. "Yes, it is."

"I'll come back tomorrow, then." She looked relieved, and Joshua watched as she walked down the path toward the main road.

He watched as she walked away, realizing that for the first time since Eve's death, he looked forward to the next day.

"You spoke to the police?" His eyes widened when Liv announced she'd been to the police station before driving out for the weekend. It was the third such weekend she'd spent in town.

She frowned, reaching for a glass of iced tea. "Yes, of course. How else would we get any further with the case?"

He sat down, his head spinning. "You don't think there was anything wrong with what I told you, do you?"

"About Rebecca's life here? No, of course not. That's not for us to judge, though. The police know what to look for. We might overlook something important that the police can do something with. They're the experts."

It didn't sit well with him. "If that's what you think is best."

"Don't you want to know what happened to Rebecca?"

Joshua clenched his teeth, reminding himself to speak gently. It wasn't always easy for him—not at all like he used to be, when he was young and hadn't yet lost everyone he ever cared for. "Of course, I do. It's just that I don't believe anything that happened here could have contributed to her loss. Telling the police implies that Rebecca did something wrong."

"No, it doesn't. That wasn't what I meant, at all. She was a victim, here."

"She was a victim where she lived with you, too."

Her eyes narrowed. Joshua sensed the anger simmering just under the surface. "I guess I was wrong. You're not committed to finding the truth."

He gaped at her. "How can you say that?" In the days they'd spent together, Liv had never spoken crossly with him. It was a surprise. Her eyes flashed, her cheeks flushed. In the back of his mind, Joshua reflected on how she looked prettier than ever. "Our ways aren't your ways. We don't look for retribution. We forgive."

"Can you honestly forgive the person who butchered your sister?"

He winced. "Please, don't use that word."

"Using it or not using it doesn't change the truth. She was butchered. With an knife. In her bedroom, where she should have felt safest. It makes no sense. I need to know. I need to." Her eyes filled with tears. His heart softened.

"I'm sorry. Please, don't cry." His arms ached to hold her, comfort her. Only the reminder of how dangerous touching her would be kept him away.

"I won't cry." She was stubborn, determined. Her shoulders

squared, and she took a long gulp of tea. When she returned the glass to the tray, she was visibly calmer. "I'm sorry I lost my temper. You have to understand how compelled I feel to learn why this happened. I loved her—I still do. More than that, too. If there's no reason behind this…if it was just a random thing…it could happen to me. It could happen to anyone. I can't go on thinking that. I'll go crazy."

Joshua sighed, seeing things from her point of view. She was right, of course. He couldn't tell her what to give to the police or withhold from them, since their worlds were so different. It was no wonder she only slept soundly when she visited for the weekend.

They fell silent. He was at a loss for what to say. They'd never exchanged cross words before.

A knock at the front door jarred them both, breaking the silence. They looked at each other. Panic swept through Joshua's heart. Who could it be? The Elders, maybe? He'd known it was wrong to have her with him, yet he'd invited her back time and again. It was only right that they should visit. They would probably reprimand him…or worse, if they saw the Englischer sitting in his living room.

"Are you all right?" Liv asked.

"Fine. Fine." He shook himself, then stood and crossed the room. There was no choice but to accept his punishment, no matter what it was.

He breathed a sigh of relief on opening the door to find not the Elders of the Ordung, but his friend, Adam. Behind Adam stood Ruth, his wife. Adam smiled his usual broad, friendly smile. Joshua noticed, though, that there was a hint of sadness in his friend's eyes ever since word of Rebecca's death had reached the community. There was a time when Adam and he would have been brothers-in-law. While Adam had married, Joshua knew all too well how difficult it was to let go of love even after being parted.

"Are you well?" Adam asked.

"Oh, fine, thank you. Only surprised to see you." He noticed Ruth looking rather furtive, glancing up at him under lowered brows.

"Ruth pointed out today that it had been a while since we last visited." Joshua glanced at Ruth again, hearing her husband's words but knowing the meaning behind them. She wanted to see if the rumors were true, if he was really entertaining an Englischer. Adam had likely brought her along to show solidarity, to prove he wouldn't shun his friend no matter what was said about him.

"I'm busy at the moment," he said, feeling intensely ridiculous. The voice he heard behind him made him feel even worse.

"I'm going to go, Joshua." Liv smiled at him, then at Adam and Ruth. "You have company, and I have some work to do at my hotel."

It was out, then. Joshua appreciated the way Liv made it clear she was staying elsewhere.

"Adam and Ruth Hertzler, this is Liv Roberts. She lived with Rebecca."

"Oh." Adam looked stunned, but extended his hand to shake hers. Ruth did not, Joshua noticed. He wondered at her judgmental reaction. Why was she behaving that way?

Joshua invited the Hertzlers in, closing the door behind Liv as she went to her car. He knew there would be questions to answer when she returned the following day.

And there were. From the moment she stepped inside the house, she peppered him with them. "Was that the Adam you spoke of? The one Rebecca wanted to marry? When did he marry Ruth? Did Rebecca know Ruth? What did they think of each other? How did Adam react when he heard Rebecca died?"

"Slow down, please" Joshua held up one hand to signal her to stop. "I can only answer one question at a time."

Liv's shoulders slumped. She sat down, looking spent. "Sorry, but I've been going crazy since yesterday. It's not as if I can call you on the phone."

He chuckled. "That's true." He then thought back to her questions. "Yes, that was the same Adam, of course. He married Ruth around a year after Rebecca left, maybe a little less than that. His parents had always wanted him to make a good match, and Ruth was the girl they'd had their eye on for a long time. She came from a much better family than ours." He tried to keep the bitterness in his heart from leaking out into his words, but it was nearly impossible.

"Go on," Liv urged. He remembered it was her job to be so unceasingly inquisitive, and he indulged her.

"The girls knew of each other. They weren't friendly, but then a lot of the girls weren't friendly with Rebecca because of the family stigma. I don't think it was anything personal. Her parents might have warned her against being too friendly with my sister. To Rebecca, she was one of the others…as most of the girls were. The ones who watched and whispered, but never approached. If you know what I mean."

Liv winced. "I hate to think of her feeling so lonely. Now I understand why she made it a point to be inclusive. She was friendly toward everyone, all the time."

"I guess even from pain; good things can result." They both smiled. It was a little comfort, at least.

"How did Adam react to the news of Rebecca's death?"

Joshua thought back on it. "I wasn't there when he found out. He came to me when he heard. He was upset, understandably. As everyone was. It's funny, how kind and forgiving everyone was when they heard she was gone. They should have been so kind when she was alive, and here. Maybe she wouldn't have left." Maybe she wouldn't have died. He couldn't help seeing it that way.

"It might have been kindness toward me, too," he mused. "I think everyone felt sorry when they found out I lost someone else."

He never spoke of Eve. He never made mention of her or said her name. Somehow, it felt like the right time. "I lost my wife a year ago."

She didn't gasp or even look surprised. He thought she might have been waiting for him to tell the story. She had a gentle, understanding way about her. She wouldn't press him for information, or make him tell her anything that might be painful. She only waited for him to continue.

"Eve was a special person. I think the two of you would have Gotten along very well. You remind me of her in some ways. She was a good listener. She had a kind heart. She was patient with me. She was due to have a baby. We'd been married for nearly three years before Gott blessed us. It felt like a miracle." He remembered how happy they'd been; how much hope they'd had for the future. Gott had heard their prayers and was blessing their love.

"It was a difficult time for her, though. I took her to the Englischer doctors when it didn't seem as though she progressed well. She had a lot of pain, was always ill. More ill than seemed normal—even the other women in the community thought so, the ones who had children of their own. The doctors told us it would be a complicated pregnancy, and that once the baby was born, it would be wise for us to not have any other children."

"She was still happy, though. Still glad to have at least one child to love. She stayed cheerful, did as much as she could around the farm. Toward the end, the doctor made her stay in bed all day."

A lump formed in his throat. He waited until it passed, then said all he could say without breaking down. "I lost them both." He couldn't describe the horror of the birth; the agony Eve had gone through. The sound of her screams echoed in his ears for weeks, months afterward. The heart-rending pain when he heard nothing but silence after the child was born. No cry. Then, the panicked voices of the midwives. The looks on their faces when they came from the birthing room.

When he looked at Liv, she was crying. Tears streamed down her cheeks. "I had no idea. Both of them. I'm so sorry."

He nodded without speaking. They sat in silence for a long time. It felt good, sharing the story, which surprised him. He never expected to be glad he'd opened up.

She closed her laptop and pushed her chair away from her desk, frustrated. There was no concentrating on her work anymore. What was happening to her?

So many things. Her heart had never been so full, and so conflicted. It seemed like all she did lately was look forward to the weekend, when she could make the drive out to Lancaster. To be with Joshua.

It had started out as a bit of comfort, a way to ease the pain. She'd told herself she was doing him a favor, too, giving him a sense of closure. Filling in the years of blank space after Rebecca ran away. When they talked about her, sharing stories, it didn't hurt so much.

But there was more than that. She had to admit it. It was him. She wanted to see him. She wanted to help him, to heal the wounds he'd suffered. He was so noble, so stand-up, yet there was a deep core of pain. The pain of his youth, being an outcast, losing his sister, his parents, his wife and baby…there was so much to be healed. She wanted to be the one to do it.

Nothing about it made sense. He was Amish! It could never work. The more time she spent with him, the more complicated things got. She told herself this throughout the week, forbidding herself to go back. It would be the best move for both of them. She knew his life wasn't easy, that he'd probably face pushback for the time he spent with her.

It wasn't enough to keep her away, though. Every Friday afternoon, she found herself making the same drive. Every Friday evening, she saw his smiling face as he opened the door. Every Sunday, it was harder than the Sunday before to leave him.

Her cell rang. Detective Kincaide. She hadn't spoken to him since the night she called from her hotel, relaying the information Joshua gave her about Rebecca's past. Her heart leaped.

"Detective?" She heard the hope in her voice.

"Liv. I have something I think you'll be interested in. We finally tracked down security footage from the day Rebecca died. We have her on a handful of cameras. I was wondering if you could come in to take a look."

"Absolutely." Then, she looked at the pile of work on her desk. "It's going to be a late night, though."

"That's fine. You know me—I'm always here." That was true. He was a workaholic, from Liv's experience. She promised to tear through her assignments and be there as soon as possible.

Still, it was nearly nine o'clock by the time she hurried from the office. When she got off the elevator in the garage, she shivered at the eerie silence. It was virtually empty, except for her car and a handful of others. Probably security, she thought. Or housekeeping. Rarely was she ever there so late. It felt sacred, almost. Only there was a strange energy in the air which left the hair on the back of her neck standing straight up.

Knock it off, she told herself. There was no reason to act like a scared kid. She was freaking herself out for no reason. Besides, getting to the police station was paramount. She pulled her jacket tighter around her shivering body and hurried for her car, footsteps echoing off the concrete pavement.

A shuffle. She froze. There was definitely some sort of shuffling footstep. Liv held her breath, eyes darting from side to side. The shadows seemed darker, more dangerous. Anyone or anything could be hiding in them. With any sort of intent.

"Hello?" she called, the wondered why she bothered. If there were a maniac waiting for her, would they step out and introduce themselves? It was what people always did in movies, though.

Yes, and the people in movies usually got themselves killed. She snickered at her own foolishness and continued to walk toward where she remembered parking the car. It was cast in deep shadow at the far end of the level. She hurried faster, fishing around in her bag for her keys.

Why did her stomach turn to ice the closer she got to the car? Why did she feel such a feeling of dread? Liv paused, breathless. It felt as though something were holding her back. Like she wasn't supposed to go any further. But why?

Suddenly, she was struck with the certainty that something terrible was waiting for her. She couldn't have explained it if forced to do so. She only knew that the car was the last place to be. She took a single step backward, eyes trained on the back end of the vehicle—the only bit visible in the dim light.

Another shuffle. Another. The shadow around the car seemed to move. Liv's eyes flew open wide in panic. She took another step backward, afraid to turn her back on whoever it was.

"Who are you? Who's there?" Why didn't she have a weapon? The closest thing was her keyring—a lot of good that would do. Otherwise, she didn't even have a travel-sized can of hairspray.

A cloaked figure stepped out of the shadows. Liv's breath caught in her throat. There was nothing visible about them—only the black cloak, with a face concealed by a dark hood. "Speak to me," she said. "What's your name?"

They raised a hand, pulling the hood down. It was a woman. Tall, slender, with deep red hair. And crazy eyes. Eyes that flashed fire.

Liv realized with sick certainty that she'd seen those eyes before, that hair. The woman in front of her.

"Step away from my car," Liv ordered. She forced herself to sound much more brave than she actually felt. Inside, she quaked. The woman was Amish, wasn't she? Hadn't she stopped by Joshua's house once, while Liv was there? With...her husband.

It all became clear.

"Ruth?" Liv asked. The woman started, surprised to be recognized. "What do you want, Ruth?"

A smile. Even crazier than the eyes. It chilled Liv to the bone. Ruth said a single word. "Revenge." From behind her back, she pulled a knife.

Everything became clear. Images of Rebecca's dead body flashed before Liv's eyes as she screamed in terror, feet flying without her consciously telling them to. She spun on her heel, fleeing across the garage. All that mattered was getting back to the elevator. She had to put steel doors between herself and the knife, and the maniac wielding it.

She reached the doors, jamming her finger against the call button. It should be here! She screamed in her head. It wasn't. The doors remained closed.

She cast a glance over her shoulder to find Ruth gaining on her. Liv had no choice but to run. She darted away just in time to miss the swinging blade as it sliced through the air.

"Ruth, stop this!" she screamed, dashing to the other side of the level, where the stairway sat. She'd outrun Ruth there. Sheer panic drove her every thought, every move. She didn't have time to think.

Ruth was gaining. Liv nearly flew the last twenty feet, throwing herself at the door. It wasn't enough. She turned just in time to see a crazed Ruth bringing the blade down once again. Liv jumped to the side, and metal hit metal as Ruth's knife made contact with the door.

Liv kicked out instinctively, hitting Ruth in the legs. It was enough to knock the woman off-balance, and as she stumbled, the knife fell from her hands. Liv scrambled to reach it—but Ruth did the same. The two of them fought and scrapped over the weapon. Liv had fear and adrenaline on her side, but Ruth had insanity. She wrenched the knife free from Liv, then gave Liv a mighty shove, knocking her to the ground.

She advanced with a menacing smile. Liv scrambled backward until her back touched the wall. There was nowhere to go. Ruth raised the knife over her head, and Liv threw up an arm to protect herself.

"Drop the weapon!" A man's voice, echoing throughout the garage. Liv opened her eyes, which had been squeezed shut in panic. Three security guards ran toward them, weapons drawn. "Put your hands in the air where we can see them!"

Ruth's face fell, as did the knife when she dropped it on the concrete. It rang with a hollow sound. She raised her hands into the air. One of the guards took her by the arms, pulling her aside.

Liv wanted to speak. She wanted to ask what happened, how they found her. All she could do was shake from head to toe. She couldn't even cry. One of the guards helped her to her feet and assured her the police were on their way. "We saw everything on the security feed," he explained. "That's how we found you." She gave the man a look of deep gratitude, and promised herself she would thank him as soon as she could speak without her teeth chattering.

***

"I don't understand. Why did she come after me?" Liv sat at the station with a cup of coffee in her hands, which still shook somewhat from time to time as the shock wore off. What a night. What a couple of months.

Detective Kincaide shrugged. "I really couldn't tell you why. The worst part is, I don't think she could, either. Nothing she did made sense. Maybe, in some part of her twisted mind, she linked you and Rebecca together."

"That's another thing I don't understand. Why did she kill Rebecca in the first place? She didn't tell me anything, and Rebecca never mentioned her. She never mentioned anybody, though, so I guess that doesn't mean anything." She'd been at the station for nearly two hours, giving statements, answering questions, crying. She'd done a lot of crying. It was almost midnight, and still she had no answers.

Kincaide looked over her shoulder with a sort of smile on his face. "Now that we're all here, I can tell you what happened." Liv looked over her shoulder and nearly burst out into fresh tears when she recognized Joshua walking toward them.

She stood, turning to face him. "What are you doing here?" she asked, beyond delighted. He didn't answer at first. Instead, he wrapped her in his arms and held her for a long, silent moment. Liv leaned against him, realizing for the first time how much she had wanted to be near him—and how much she'd wished he were with her as she went through the trauma with Ruth over and over again.

"How are you?" he asked, pulling back, looking at her very critically.

"I'll be all right," she assured him with a smile. "I mean it. I'm not hurt." Then, she laughed softly. "Look at you! In the big city!"

"Not many things could bring me here," he admitted, starting meaningfully at Liv. Her heart nearly burst from happiness—none of it made any sense. They didn't go together. Yet nothing could have stopped her from rejoicing at the knowledge that he wanted her in some small way.

"Now that Mr. Blough is here, we can get started. Thank you for coming, Joshua. I know it wasn't easy for our detectives to convince you."

"Once they told me it was for Liv, I got in the car." Liv blushed, and the two of them sat beside each other at Kincaide's desk.

"I think the detectives told you, Joshua, that it was Ruth Hertzler who attacked Liv earlier tonight."

"They did, but why would Ruth do something like that?" He looked at Liv. She shrugged.

"I didn't know her," she murmured.

The detective nodded. "No, you didn't know her. And she didn't know you. But she knew Rebecca—or, rather, she knew Rebecca was having an affair with her husband."

Liv's jaw hit the floor. "Rebecca? Having an affair?"

"I don't believe Adam would go outside his marriage like that," Joshua protested. "That isn't like him."

"I respect your way of life very much, Joshua, but I can assure you that even the most pious person falls victim to love. And that's what it appeared to be between Adam and Rebecca. Not just an affair." He stared hard at Joshua. "Rebecca told me the two of them were in love, and would have been married if things had gone differently."

The comment subdued Joshua. "That's right," he said softly.

Kincaide sat down. "According to Ruth—mind you, we're taking a lot of what she says with a grain of salt until we can corroborate with Adam—Rebecca and Adam had an affair for over a year."

Liv gasped. "How is that possible? I would have known! She must be wrong—you said it yourself, she's crazy enough that you can't take her word for it. She's making it all up."

He turned to her. "Did Rebecca attend a teaching conference in Strasburg a little over a year ago?"

Liv thought back, and nodded slowly. Joshua was nearly apoplectic. "She was so close, and she never thought to visit me?"

"I'm sure she thought you would reject her—and remember, she didn't know your parents were gone. It was too risky." Liv answered almost out of reflex, not thinking much about her words. She only wanted to assure Joshua. In reality, her brain teemed with questions. How could Rebecca have kept a secret like that? Then again, she'd kept her entire life a secret for so long. What was one more secret on top of that?"

"It appears as though Adam was there on some business—buying farming equipment, something like that. He ran into her in a coffee shop."

"Oh, my God," Liv whispered. She knew Rebecca well enough to know her friend would have considered it Fate. The love of her life walking into the very coffee shop she sat in.

"After that, they got together once every few weeks."

"You did not know this?" Joshua asked Liv.

"She would spend weekends away sometimes, or just the night. She always told me she was visiting friends."

Kincaide nodded. "We ran the financials on her credit cards. Turns out, she'd been charging to a certain hotel. The clerk described a man bearing a strong resemblance to Adam Hertzler as the man Rebecca stayed with during every visit."

"I can't believe it." Liv sat back in the chair with a defeated sigh. It was right in front of her face, and she never saw it. "The two of us…we were close, but we had our own lives, too. I never thought much of her being away, since she had so many friends. She was the type of person who would drop everything if somebody was having trouble. She'd go right to them—and I know she was going to them, and not some boyfriend. I don't want you thinking she was the kind of person to do this all the time."

"On the contrary," Kincaide said, "it sounds like Rebecca was a stand-up person. When faced with the love of her life, she couldn't resist. Neither could Adam."

"How does Ruth tie into this?" Joshua asked.

"One night, she followed him. She actually got into a cab to do it —that's how determined she was to find out why her husband disappeared the way he did. She saw Rebecca. They'd known each other as children, of course, being part of the same community. Ruth was under no illusions. She knew her husband loved Rebecca when they were younger. When she married him, it was a dream come true for her. She was convinced she could make him love her the way he loved Rebecca. And after a few years, she'd thought she succeeded. But there was Rebecca, again."

"She went crazy," Kincaide continued. "Obsessed. She couldn't confront Adam about it, since she was afraid he would leave her. Instead, she turned her energy to hating Rebecca. She found her address—they were writing letters, too, it turns out. She read them, got the address from one of the envelopes, and took the train into the city. She told Adam she was visiting cousins in Baltimore."

Liv covered her face with her hands, absorbing the horrible information. Joshua spoke up. "I don't understand how a woman in our clothing, the plain clothing of our people, escaped notice in the city."

Kincaide chuckled grimly. "You'd be surprised what happens in the city that nobody seems to notice. A woman in a cloak isn't such a strange sight."

"He's right," Liv admitted.

"She carried a big bag, too, to hide the craving knife."

"Was that…the one she had in the garage…was that the one she used?" Liv asked in a small, strangled voice.

"We're running forensics tests on it right now, but preliminary tests tell us it was," he said, in a kind voice. Liv let out a low moan.

When she calmed down, Kincaide added, "She was the woman I wanted you to look at, Liv. The one on the security cameras. She followed Rebecca around on the day of the murder—always from a safe distance, always out of sight. Rebecca never noticed her."

It all seemed too sad and surreal to be true. Her best friend, hiding a double life. How could she have fessed up, though? Telling Liv about Adam would have meant spilling the beans on her entire history—a history she clearly wanted very much to forget.

"If only she had told me," Liv mused. "If I had only known about him, I might have…I don't know…talked her out of it. I hate that she went through it all by herself."

"Unless my sister changed a great deal—and from what you've told me, she didn't—she was too stubborn to listen. You couldn't have talked her out of it." Joshua was right, Liv knew, but it didn't stop her from asking "what if". She'd be asking it forever, she suspected.

"That's it, then," Kincaide announced, standing up. "We have what we need. Liv, you're free to go. Thank you for everything you gave us to help with this."

"Thank you." She hugged him, knowing it wasn't the last time they would see each other—there would surely be a trial, and she wouldn't miss it for anything—but there was a certain feeling of finality. They had gotten what they'd worked for. They knew who ended Rebecca's life.

"You'll need a ride back to the farm, of course," the detective said to Joshua. "Unless you've be willing to accept accommodation for the night, here in town. Nothing too fancy, but I guess that wouldn't bother you too much."

Joshua chuckled at the joke—Liv was glad to see he was in good humor—then grew serious. "Will Adam be here soon?"

"He should be here any time. We'll be taking statements from him for hours."

Joshua nodded. "Then I will stay in the city, as long as your officers promise to bring me here to see him in the morning."

"That can be arranged." Kincaide made a phone call, getting a room together at a local hotel for Joshua. Liv turned to him, one eyebrow raised.

"So, staying in the big city?" she asked, smirking.

"I feel it's worth the exception," he replied.

"Why is seeing Adam so important to you?" she asked. "Important enough for you to spend the night in an Englischer hotel?"

"I want him to know he isn't alone."

Liv's heart went out to him. He was the noblest person she'd ever known. "Even though he went against your laws? Even though he indirectly led to Rebecca's murder?"

Joshua stroked his beard, thinking it through. Then, he nodded. "Even though. If there's one thing being my father's son taught me, it's that old sins must be forgiven. They can't be held against a person for their entire lives. Besides, if I were to hold Adam's sins against him, it would only be harmful to myself. That's why forgiveness is so important."

"I feel as though there's so much I can learn from you," Liv said, marveling at Joshua's depth of compassion.

"I have all the time in the world to teach you," he murmured with a shy smile.

"I can't get enough of these cookies."

"Maybe I shouldn't have given you the recipe. I'll have to get these pants let out if I gain any more weight."

Liv laughed. "As if my cooking was so good." She brought a tin for him, as she always did when she visited. Lancaster had become a second home to her in the months since Ruth's attack. She spent less and less time in Philadelphia.

"You said there was something you wanted to talk about," he said. Her heart skipped a beat. This was it. How would he react?

"I've decided to move here, permanently."

His eyes brightened. "That's great news!" His voice was warm, enthused.

"It's more than that, though. See, I know you've been going through trouble of your own, thanks to me."

"Nothing I can't handle," he assured her.

"I don't want you to go through that because of me, though. I think we should stop seeing each other this way."

Joshua gasped. "What? Why? When you're moving out here, especially? Why would you do that?"

It was the reaction she'd secretly hoped for. He wanted to be with her as much as she wanted to be with him.

"I said this way. Not entirely. Just this way."

He frowned. "I don't understand. You want to sneak around?" His voice was low, almost a whisper.

"No! I want to join your faith."

It was like she'd dropped a bomb on him. He looked completely stunned. His mouth hung open. "You want to join us? To be Amish?"

"Yes. That's what I want, more than anything. I could sit here and tell you all about everything you've given me, everything you've done for me. The peace I feel here—not just when I'm with you, but when I'm in your world. I could tell you how right this feels, how it's like I've been missing something for years and finally found it. I could do all of that, and I will over time. There's one real, driving force, though."

"What's that?" he asked.

"I want to be with you. For real."

For one breathless moment, she wasn't sure how he would react. His face was blank, like it hadn't caught up with his brain. Then... he smiled.

"It won't be easy," he warned.

"What is?" she asked. "I'll have you to help me. That's all I need." She reached for him, and he closed a hand over hers. It was a start.

***

A year passed. It was late winter again, just as it had been when Liv first went to the door at the end of the dirt lane. When she first met Joshua, and they started on a journey together which neither of them could have predicted.

Joshua entered the kitchen, where cookies were just being pulled from the oven. "Sugar cookies," he said with a smile. "How do you always know my favorite?"

"It's not difficult to remember," Liv said with a smile. She went by Olivia in Amish circles, but Joshua still called her Liv when they were alone. Just another thing that had changed about her over the last tumultuous year.

She smiled to herself when she thought about the sleepless nights she'd spent, wondering what her true path in life was to be. If she were meant to be a reporter in Philadelphia, living the life of a single girl in the city, why did she feel such a pull toward the Amish she'd met? Why did her life seem so empty and meaningless, when it had seemed so full before? Why did she miss Joshua with every fiber of her being?

She had missed him. She'd thought about him nearly constantly, to the point where her heart ached. She would visit as much as she could, but even that wasn't enough to sate her desperate heart. It was enough to get Joshua into trouble, though, and his visits with the strange Englischer girl brought him under scrutiny. He'd been called up before the Elders.

When he'd told her of this development, Liv's mind was made up.

She approached him with her idea, and he naturally thought it was insane at first. But she'd worn him down, convincing him how deeply committed she was to making good on her new life.

"You'll have to do a lot of talking with the Bishop," he'd said, staring very seriously into her eyes. "He will want to know everything about you, to judge how serious you are in your commitment. You'll have to be baptized, too. Once you are, there's no going back. This isn't the sort of thing you can choose one day and toss aside the next."

Liv had heard the truth in his words—he meant the faith, yes, but he also meant himself. For in her decision to join the faith, she was committing herself to him, as well. He was a major reason for her choice. He knew it, and he didn't object, which made her heart take flight. If he didn't have feelings for her, he wouldn't be so willing to accept the idea of her joining. He was afraid she would leave him, when leaving was the furthest thing from her mind.

He hadn't been joking about the Bishop, either. Liv had nearly sweated bullets when called to stand before him. For three hours he had questioned her, very gently but very seriously. Did she understand the gravity of her decision? What made her wish to join? What would happen if she decided one day that she no longer wished to be part of the faith? Was she really ready to leave her worldly possessions behind, in order to embrace the plain life of the Amish?

She had assured him of her seriousness, and he had seemed impressed with her determination. She had never wanted anything more. Once her mind had been made up, everything went crystal clear. She would miss nothing about her life that couldn't be replaced in some other, better way. So what if there would be no internet, no movies, no cable, none of life's little conveniences? She would have so much more. Peace. Serenity. Love. Faith. The things she never had in her Englisch life.

How funny. Rebecca had made the exact opposite move, years earlier. Both of them gave up everything they'd ever known. Both of them knew they would find happiness—only Liv's chances were better than Rebecca's, since she had Joshua.

He was so different from the man he'd been when they first met. Of course, he was still warm, generous, noble and kind. He still understood Liv's heart better than anybody else. The layer of ice around his heart had thawed, though. He seemed younger, more lighthearted. He looked forward to the future. He wasn't alone anymore. He laughed a lot, and his laugh reminded Liv of Rebecca. They had such a similar sense of humor.

It wasn't always easy, the transition to a new life—especially one so drastically different from the one she'd always known. With Joshua's help, and her ever-growing faith in Gott, it got easier every day.

As she finished fixing supper for her husband, Liv wondered at the way Rebecca's death had changed life in such unpredictable ways. She'd brought her best friend and brother together; the way they were meant to be. She'd helped her best friend discover a life and a faith much more satisfying than anything she'd known before.

Liv stroked her distended belly and felt the baby kick, she smiled in wonder of the new life growing inside her. Liv knew her life was now complete – her perfect husband, growing faith and the new family on its way…

I would like to thank you for taking the time to read my book. I really hope that you enjoyed it as much as I enjoyed writing it.

I have been writing Amish books for Amazon for almost two years now, almost exclusively on Kindle. However, due to growing demand I managed to get the majority of my titles available in paperback versions. There is a list of all of my kindle books below, bit by bit they are ALL going to be released in paperback so please keep checking them.

If you feel able I would love for you to give the book a short review on Amazon.

If you want to keep up to date with all of my latest releases then please like my Facebook Page, simply search for Hannah Schrock author.

Many thanks once again, all my love.

Hannah.

LATEST BOOKS

DON'T MISS HANNAH'S BRAND NEW *MAMMOTH AMISH MEGA BOOK* - 20 Stories in one box set.

Mammoth Amish Romance Mega Book 20 books in one set

Outstanding value for 20 books

OTHER BOX SETS

Amish Romance Mega book **(contains many of Hannah's older titles)**
Amish Love and Romance Collection

MOST RECENT SINGLE TITLES

The Orphan's Amish Teacher
The Mysterious Amish Suicide
The Pregnant Amish Quilt Maker
The Amish Caregiver
The Amish Detective: The King Family Arsonist
The Amish Gift
Becoming Amish
The Amish Foundling Girl
The Heartbroken Amish Girl
The Missing Amish Girl
Amish Joy
The Amish Detective

Amish Double

The Burnt Amish Girl

AMISH ROMANCE SERIES

AMISH HEARTACHE

AMISH REFLECTIONS: AMISH ANTHOLOGY COLLECTION

MORE AMISH REFLECTIONS : ANOTHER AMISH ANTHOLOGY COLLECTION

THE AMISH WIDOW AND THE PREACHER'S SON

AN AMISH CHRISTMAS WITH THE BONTRAGER SISTERS

A BIG BEAUTIFUL AMISH COURTSHIP

AMISH YOUNG SPRING LOVE BOX SET

AMISH PARABLES SERIES BOX SET

AMISH HEART SHORT STORY COLLECTION

AMISH HOLDUP

AN AMISH TRILOGY BOX SET

AMISH ANGUISH

SHORT AMISH ROMANCE STORIES

AMISH BONTRAGER SISTERS 2 - THE COMPLETE SECOND SEASON

AMISH BONTRAGER SISTERS - THE COMPLETE FIRST SEASON

THE AMISH BROTHER'S BATTLE

AMISH OUTSIDER

AMISH FORGIVENESS AND FRIENDSHIP

THE AMISH OUTSIDER'S LIE

AMISH VANITY

AMISH NORTH

AMISH YOUNG SPRING LOVE SHORT STORIES SERIES

THE AMISH BISHOP'S DAUGHTER

THE AMISH BONTRAGER SISTERS SHORT STORIES SERIES

THE AMISH PARABLES SERIES

THE AMISH BUILDER

THE AMISH PRODIGAL SON

AMISH PERSISTENCE

THE AMISH GOOD SAMARITAN

Also Out Now:

The Amish Caregiver

If there's one thing Eve has always been good at, it's caring for those around her. Whether it's her family, neighbors in the Amish community in which she lives, or even the animals on her farm. Eve is first to offer help thanks to her kind and giving heart.

When a terrible storm causes a young Englischer named Oliver to crash his car on the road outside her house, it's Eve's instinct to act as caregiver. As she nurses him back to health, she finds herself growing attached to him - but her heart is torn apart when he has to leave.

Will Eve ever be able to put her feelings for Oliver aside once he goes back to his life in the Englisch world? Or does Gott have a grander plan for the two of them?

Here is a Taster:

"Mamm, you must try to drink some more broth."

Eve sighed as her mother turned her head from the spoon offered her. She was eating less and less every day. Eve prayed, as she had so many times a day, that Gott would spare her. The prayer was a constant one. Almost like breathing. In and out. Spare my mother. In and out. Spare my mother.

For years, Eve had been caring for everyone and everything around her. Her parents would smile lovingly whenever she brought home a bird with a broken wing, or insisted a stray cat stay with them. Sometimes it would become too much even for them, loving people though they were. "This house has become a zoo," her Mamm would say with a furrowed brow. But as soon as she saw the look of pure hope on her daughter's face, Ruth Lantz would smile. She had known how rare it was for a person to be so totally dedicated to the welfare of others.

"Gott has a special plan for all of our lives," Ruth would say, pulling Eve toward her for an affectionate hug. "I believe He wishes for you to help others when they are most in need."

Eve had taken that to heart. Whenever a member of their community became ill, she was the first at the door to offer her services. Even if it was something as simple as helping with chores so the family didn't fall behind, or preparing food to take to the sick person. She had helped nurse little Noah Yoder back to health when he had a grievous cough and fever.

Perhaps if she had been born into the world of the Englisch, she would have studied to be a doctor. She thought about that sometimes, what it would be like to learn all the mysteries of the body and how to heal a person's every illness. How exciting that might be. But only Gott should know such things. He knew best. It was merely up to people to do His work. Too much knowledge, and a person might begin to think they knew better than Gott.

Still, as she sat at her dying mother's bedside, Eve wished there were more she could do.

Mamm was holding up well, though. She was bearing her illness with the same strength and faith which had carried her throughout life. She was never without a kind word on her lips or a prayer in her heart. Oftentimes, she and Eve would pray together.

Eve wiped her mother's brow. She had fallen asleep, her chest rising and falling in shallow breaths. It was only a matter of time.

She took the opportunity to fetch a fresh basin of water and clean towels. Downstairs, her Daed was sitting by the hearth. It was unusual for him to be indoors in the early afternoon—normally, he would have been outside with his son, Caleb, and the farm hands.

"Daed?" Eve placed a gentle hand on her father's shoulder. He seemed to have aged years in only the few short weeks since receiving the news of his wife's cancer. "Can I do anything for you?"

He did not look up at her, but gently patted her hand. "No, thank you, dochder. You are doing so much already. It is a comfort to me that you care so well for your mother in these final days." So he had accepted the fact of his wife's impeding death. For days, he hadn't. He had prayed more fervently than all the rest, sure that Gott would hear him and cure his beloved wife.

"Perhaps you should go and speak with her," Eve said. "She is sleeping at the moment, but she never sleeps for very long. The pain is too great. Every time she moves it wakes her."

He let out a shuddering sigh, and Eve wondered if she had misspoken. For some reason, though she had always thought of her father as the strongest man in the world, it appeared as though she was even stronger than him. It was a strange feeling.

"I will see her shortly. I must go out and help Caleb with the plowing." He sighed. He patted Eve's shoulder. "You are a blessing to us."

Eve didn't see it that way at all. She was merely doing what she felt compelled to do. Her parents had worked hard for years to ensure that Eve and her younger brother lived a good life and had their needs met. The least Eve could do was to care for her mother.

Neighbors visited throughout the day, checking on Ruth and asked how Eve was getting along in her caregiving. "You must take time to rest," Mrs. Lapp said, holding a hand to Eve's forehead as though to check for temperature. Eve only smiled and assured her family's closest neighbor that she was doing well and getting all the rest she needed. Inside, she reminded herself that she didn't need as much rest as an older person might. She was young, only eighteen, and strong. She had the fortitude to spend the long, sleepless nights by her mother's bedside in case she needed anything. Ruth had been moved to Eve's bedroom, so she might be more comfortable and not disturb her husband, who needed to be up before the sun to attend to the needs of the farm.

After a while, it was just Eve and Ruth again. The others were kind to visit, but they had their own families and homes to attend to. The evening meal would have to be prepared.

"Eve." It was a thin whisper, one which Eve had to lean close to hear.

"Yes, Mamm?"

"I am glad you are my dochder. You have a gift for caring. Use that to help others, but take care of yourself, too. Do not wear yourself down. And always put Gott first."

Eve nodded, tears filling her eyes. Her mother's breathing had become more labored. Just the act of speaking so few words had exhausted her.

She took the chance, running downstairs and out the door to call for her father and brother. The time had come—somewhere inside, she knew it.

By the time they reached Ruth's bedside, it was too late.

Two Years Later

Eve jumped at the sound of thunder. She peered out the window over the sink, where she washed the supper dishes. Rain fell so hard and fast; it was impossible to see anything but sheets of water.

The storm was bound to be a terrible one. All day, dark, angry clouds had raced across the sky. The air had fairly crackled with electricity, somehow feeling heavier. Anyone accustomed to summer storms knew there was a strong one brewing.

The thunder boomed again, this time accompanied by a zigzagging bolt of lightning. Eve's heart raced, though she knew she was far too old to be afraid of a silly storm. She would have felt better had her father and brother been inside the house with her, but the odds were they were in the barn, tending to the horses. The animals became so easily spooked at times like that.

She dried her hands on a towel, then took the chance to stepping outside to the covered porch. Rain pounded on the roof over her head, sounding like thousands of thudding hooves. A stampede. It was almost enough to make her cover her ears. She narrowed her blue eyes, hoping to catch a glimpse of her father or Caleb in the downpour. She could see nothing in the heavy rain.

She looked down at the ground beyond the porch. Water was already rising. This is terrible, she thought. Her garden might be drowned, to say nothing of the crops. She hoped it was a strong but fast-moving storm.

A sound floated to her ears just above the cacophony of thudding rain. Even looked back out toward the barn. There was someone there, waving his arms. Daed. He needed her help.

Thinking nothing of herself, Eve took off at a run. Instantly, she was soaked to the skin thanks to the downpour. She shielded her eyes from the driving rain, praying nobody was hurt.

"What is it?" she yelled, hoping to be heard over the storm.

"The horses! We weren't finished bringing them in before it started!" Sure enough, four of them were running loose in the paddock, terrified by the crashing thunder. "We have to get them into the barn!"

Eve nodded, turning to the paddock fence. It was dangerous to approach a spooked horse, but she had built quite a rapport with their horses over the years. She had a gentle nature which they responded to. Reminding herself to be calm, she shimmied through a small opening in the gate.

"Come, Lady," she said, holding one hand to her favorite mare. "Come."

The horse sniffed her hand, and she patted its head. Taking the reins, she led her to the barn, where Caleb was waiting.

They took turns, she and Caleb, calming then leading the horses inside. Rain ran down her face and beat down her back. Her shoes sank into the mud, making it more difficult to even lift her feet from the ground. It was hard work to say the least. Eve wiped water from her eyes, looking forward to getting back inside where it was dry and comfortable. The hem of her dress was covered in mud. It would have to be soaked, along with her muddy stockings.

A bolt of lightning cut across the sky, making the horse Eve was leading rear up on its hind legs. For a brief moment, she was terrified by the thrashing hooves. Then she remembered to keep calm, that nothing would happen to her as long as she remained calm and loving toward the animal.

Daed made a move toward them, as though to help her, but Eve held him off. It would only upset the horse more if he felt as though he were being surrounded.

"Peace, Clover! Peace! There, there." She ran a gentle hand over the horse's muzzle, scratching him behind the ears. Then she continued to lead him the extra hundred yards to the barn while her father closed the paddock gate.

"Eve, the nerve you have!" Daed laughed. "You might have

missed your calling. A horse trainer might have been what you were meant to be!"

Eve blushed. She didn't think much of her accomplishment. She just seemed to know what the horse needed.

"Get back to the house," he said, frowning. "I do not want you to become ill, out in the storm this way. I disliked even having to ask you to help."

"That is what I am here for, Daed," she said, smiling. "We work as a family, right?" She turned away and dared the walk back to the house. She didn't run—it was pointless, as she was already soaked through. It was difficult enough to keep her footing, besides, in the slippery mud.

The rain had let up a bit, allowing Eve a better look around the land. Her family's home wasn't set far back from the road. And out there, just beyond the fence separating their land from the neighbors, was a pair of blinking lights.

Eve stopped, waiting to see if they would move. It seemed as though a car was stuck, perhaps in mud off the side of the road. Now the rain didn't matter—it fell on her head, trickled down her face, but it was no matter. She wanted to see whether the driver would leave the car, stopped as it was by the big tree.

Daed and Caleb were still in the barn. Eve went alone to see whether the driver was in need of assistance—her father and brother were strong. Maybe they could push the car out of the mud. She ran to the road, slipping with every step.

When she reached the road, she saw a set of dark marks leading to where the car had settled. As though the driver lost control and the car spun. Eve ran to the car, now fearful. A man was slumped against the wheel, blood trickling down his head.

She looked up, screaming Caleb's name. When he appeared outside the barn, she screamed again. "He needs help!" She tried the door, pulling the handle, but it wouldn't budge.

Moments later, Daed and Caleb came on the run. They assessed the situation, trying all of the doors on the car. It took the two of them working in unison to pull the door beside the driver open.

Eve trotted behind them as they carried the man to the house. He was unconscious, his head still bleeding. They took him to the spare bedroom, laying him carefully down.

"See if he has other injuries," Eve fretted behind them.

"Wait outside," her father ordered. "We will check him over. I do not wish for you to see anything improper." Eve stood outside the room, frustrated. She had no desire to do anything except help the injured man. She listened while the two men checked his arms, legs, beneath his shirt for bleeding or bruising.

"He seems all right, come in." Eve returned. "There is a cut on his forehead, and a few additional scratches. No broken bones, it seems." Caleb stood back, pondering. He might have wounds inside, though, might he not?"

Daed nodded, grim. "Go down to the telephone shanty, Caleb. Call the hospital, ask for an ambulance. He should be looked at by a doctor."

Caleb left in a hurry. Eve saw him running for the road through the bedroom window. The rain was still coming down in buckets, the sky growing darker as night approached.

"I'll get towels, Daed. Some clothing from Caleb's room, maybe? He is shivering."

"Yes, do. I will change him. Caleb can help me when he returns."

Eve dashed around the house, getting things together. She also poured hot water into a basin, to wash the man's forehead. There was blood all down the side of his face, too.

By the time she returned to the bedroom, Caleb was running up the stairs. He was winded, and bent at the waist to catch his breath.

"No...phone...lines are down." He panted for air.

"The phone isn't working?" Daed asked. Caleb shook his head.

"The lines have been brought down by the storm. I cannot reach the hospital. I don't believe an ambulance could make it here, even if I got through. Trees are blocking the road as far as the eye can see, in both directions."

The three of them stared at each other, then one by one they turned to the man in the bed.

Daed spoke up. "I suppose he will need to stay with us until we can make it through."

Eve left the bedroom once again while Daed and Caleb dressed the man in dry clothing. He was nearly Caleb's size, so his clothing would fit near enough. While they worked, Eve changed out of her own wet clothing, setting her muddy dress to soak before returning with an oil lamp to the spare bedroom.

He was still unconscious. Eve sat by his side, placing a wash cloth in the water basin before applying the cloth to the stranger's face. There was a lot of dried blood, and Caleb had to empty the basin and refill it before everything was washed away. Then she sat, quiet. She wondered about him. Where had he come from? Where was he going when his car crashed?

"I suppose we should take shifts," Paul Lantz suggested. Eve looked up at her Daed, eyes wide.

"I will take the first shift," she said, almost out of instinct. It was part of her, the need to care for others. It was that need which had brought her to the stranger's car—the need to know whether there was any way to help the man.

He shook his head, his long beard shaking back and forth with him. "I don't think that would be a wise idea, leaving you alone with a stranger—an Englischer, at that."

Eve smiled. "I don't think any harm will come to me. The man is unconscious. He can't move, let alone assault me in any way."

He laughed at her saucy tone. "Fair enough."

"I will take the second shift," Caleb offered. Eve promised to wake him in three hours, though she thought she might allow him to sleep a little longer. He needed the rest more than she did—everybody worked hard on a farm, but the labor of the men was more physically demanding. At least, Eve thought so. She did better with less sleep than her father or brother.

Once she was alone with him, Eve had the chance to think. Everything had happened so fast. Only an hour or so earlier, she was washing dishes and watching the storm. The storm still raged, but now she sat at the bedside of a sick man.

A sick man who happened to be very handsome.

Her cheeks flushed at the turn her thoughts had taken, but there was no denying them. With his face cleaned of blood, except for the little bit seeping through the bandage Eve applied once he was cleaned up, it was clear that he was a very nice looking man. He might have been the most handsome man she'd ever seen. There were a few nice looking young men in her community, one or two of whom she had stolen glances at during church meetings or gatherings. None of them held a candle to the stranger.

His eyes were closed, naturally, and his long, thick eyelashes fell on his cheeks. They seemed to go on forever. His jaw was firm, square. His nose was fine and straight. His hair was thick and dark, swept back from his forehead.

She looked at his eyes again, wishing they were open. Not only would that mean he was awake, naturally, but Eve would be able to see so much more of the person he was inside. It was so easy to tell what a person was like by looking into their eyes.

She wondered what color his eyes were, too.

Then, she shook herself. It was silly, having thoughts like these. Not only that, but they were bound to lead in a direction she knew she should not stray toward. She was thinking about him in a way she shouldn't think about any man, except the man she was to marry.

It was doubly wrong to think this way about an Englischer. He was from another world, far removed from the ways of the Amish like herself. His world was forbidden to her, full of temptation which would only serve to lead her away from Gott.

Still, it was nearly impossible not to be interested in him, to wish she could speak to him. All she had to do was sit by his bedside. Her mind wandered on its own.

Did he have girlfriends? She was sure he must, somebody as handsome as he was. There had to be plenty of girls all over him. She knew how free and easy girls behaved in the Englisch world. She couldn't even wear her blonde hair down in public, or leave it uncovered. Yes, the girls were probably crazy about him.

She told herself it wasn't wrong to have these thoughts, since the stranger was sick and unconscious. As long as they didn't go any further, she wouldn't have anything to feel guilty about.

He stirred fretfully. She leaned over him, placing a hand on his forehead to soothe him. She wanted to be sure he wasn't running a fever, too. She knew that some illnesses could lead to fever and infection if left unchecked. He was cool to the touch, and Eve thanked Gott for it. If he were badly injured inside, there would be nothing she could do for him.

He had a strong, fine body. It was unlikely that he worked on a farm, the way her brother did, though their builds were very much the same. He might have been an athlete. In any case, he was a very active person who took care of himself.

Not for the first time did she ask herself where he was supposed to be. She wondered if the people there were worried over him. She would have been, in their shoes, knowing he was on his way during a fierce storm. The rain still fell, and the wind had picked up. It made the windows rattle in their casements. She shuddered to think of the condition of the farm by the time the rain stopped. There would be a lot of work to do.

And there was him. The stranger. She wondered if he would be with them for very long. How long would it take before the roads were cleared? Daed and Caleb could take him to the hospital in the buggy if need be, if the telephone lines weren't up in time to call for an ambulance.

The Amish Caregiver

Also Out Now:

The Amish Detective: The King Family Arsonist

Gloria Kauffman's world has been turned upside down. Her beloved cousin, Susan King, died three days ago in a house fire which also claimed her parents and twin brothers. The entire family is in mourning, and the community is shaken to the core when the police determine the fire was an act of arson. Who would commit such a heinous crime? And who will be next?

At the service, Gloria meets Detective Paul Miller, a young man whose determination to solve the case is second only to hers. They join together to investigate the crime and develop a bond that dangers on forbidden love.

Gloria believes there's something suspicious about the crime. The King family were nothing but good, generous, pious Amish people. Who would have wanted to hurt them, and why?

It isn't long until Gloria finds out the sad, shocking and terrible truth - and that truth might come at the cost of her life.

Here is a Taster:

Gloria sat in the corner of the barn, wiping tears from her eyes as members of the Ordung filed through, one by one, to pay their respects to a beloved family.

It all seemed like a nightmare, one Gloria wished she could awaken from. The last three days had all been part of that nightmare. Everything changed the moment her family received word of the fire. By then, most of their neighbors already knew the story. Life had been spent in a haze since then.

It wasn't just the fact of the fire that worried members of the Ordung, both the communities in which she and her extended family lived. It was the way the fire took place. The police stated it was a clear case of arson, meaning that someone had deliberately started the fire which killed her aunt, uncle and three cousins in their sleep.

Neighbors were in an uproar, and rightly so. How could they protect themselves from this arsonist? Who would be next? There was no question that the act was random—the Kings had no enemies. That simply wasn't the way of the Amish. And they spent very little time outside the community, so there was only limited involvement with the Englischers in town. It wasn't plausible that some person Isaac King knew or did business with would go so far as to set fire to the home. It had to be a sad, troubled person who felt the need to hurt others.

Who would they hurt next?

It was heartbreaking, seeing the pain on the faces of friends and neighbors as they paid their respects. Isaac, a good and hardworking farmer. He had been so well-loved. Esther, always ready with a helping hand and a gentle smile. The two of them had been a strong couple, their commitment to one another second only to their commitment to Gott. There they were. Like second parents to Gloria for as long as she could remember. Both of them in their simple wooden caskets.

Then there were the other three caskets, and Gloria's heart broke a little further when she picked her cousin Susan's out from the three. Susan who was more like a sister to Gloria than a cousin. Whose loyalty and devotion never wavered. Gloria had always wanted to be more like Susan, who was endlessly patient and good to everyone she knew. She had never so much as told a lie, and now she was gone.

And the smaller caskets. Jacob and Elijah, the twins. Only ten years old. They would never grow up to be good men like their father. It seemed as though tears would never stop flowing from

Gloria's eyes.

It was worse for her mother, Uncle Isaac's younger sister. She was inconsolable—throughout the days following the fire, Gloria had woken in the middle of the night to the sound of her mother's tears. It seemed as though they might never end.

It was true that faith in Gott that helped the Amish through difficult times, but this was far beyond anything anyone had ever encountered. Not just grief, which everyone must face at one time or another, but fear of the unknown. An Amish person's life generally fell into a distinct, routine pattern. This terrible tragedy had destroyed that pattern.

Even from her quiet corner seat, Gloria overheard the grumblings of several of the community's most respected leaders. They were considering holding a meeting to form teams of men to keep watch on the homes and farms of their neighbors. Never had anything like this been considered in the past. Gloria felt somehow as though so much of what she loved about her life was slipping away. The peace, tranquility, trust. It was the same for all the others. Would they even have a decent night's sleep while waiting to see whose home was next?

"Gloria, are you well?" One of the neighbors, Mrs. Stolztfus, approached.

"As well as can be, thank you," she replied. Her heart wasn't in her words. She felt cold inside.

"Your Mamm seems to be holding up well, all things considered."

"Yes, all things considered." It wasn't in Gloria's nature to be short or sharp, especially with one of her elders, but the older woman couldn't seem to get the message that she didn't wish to speak. It was all too strenuous. Even basic conversation was too much.

"You and your cousin Susan were very close, I know. I remember when you were just little girls, running barefoot along the outside of your home."

Gloria clenched her fist to keep from crying out loud. Didn't Mrs. Stoltzfus understand she was causing pain? Maybe, one day, it would be possible to sit and think of Susan and smile. Maybe Gloria would be able to reminisce about the times she spent with her sweet cousin and remember them fondly, instead of wishing them back with all her might. If only she could go back.

Mrs. Stoltzfus clicked her tongue in sympathy. "To think of something like this happening to Isaac King, of all people. Only the most pious person anyone had ever known, and the friendliest. If it could happen to him, it could happen to any of us."

Gloria had heard it all before, whispered and murmured from one neighbor to another. She gave the same response she had for days. "We must trust in Gott."

"Of course, of course. I only wish the person responsible were caught for what they did. I'm sure it would be easier for your poor Mamm to get over the loss of her brother if she knew the person who took his life was behind bars, where he could hurt no one else."

Then, she walked away, and Gloria couldn't help but breathe a sigh of relief. She had felt suffocated by the older woman's presence. The air felt clearer, cooler.

Why did people feel the need to cloak their curiosity and own selfish need to fret and worry under the mask of care? Gloria knew her neighbor was only venting her fear, and maybe even relishing the excitement of the situation—morbid though that was. Why couldn't people behave that way amongst themselves and leave those who mourned alone with their grief?

Susan's casket. Gloria's eyes kept falling on it. She remembered the gold of Susan's hair, and the cornflower blue of her eyes. Those eyes that had laughed and sparkled, always full of joy. Gloria would never know another person like her. My life will always be a little darker, she thought.

She thought about what Mrs. Stoltzfus said, too, about Uncle Isaac's piousness and how respected and trusted he had been. It was all true, all of it, and it added just another layer to the shock and horror of the event.

If only I had visited Susan when I said I would. It was something she'd berate herself over for the rest of her life. She was sure of it. If only she hadn't been so busy getting her next quilt ready for sale, she could have spent time with her cousin before…before the fire.

I'll never make a mistake like that again. She would never pass up the opportunity to spend time with her loved ones. Nothing was more important than that. There was no guarantee that any of them would be around tomorrow. If there was nothing else to be taken from the tragedy, Gloria thought, that was lesson enough.

Her father, brothers and sisters all gathered together toward the front of the crowd, near where the caskets sat. She wondered if anyone thought it strange that she sat alone—there was no missing the eyes that had watched her throughout the day. People asking themselves why she sat alone. If they had bothered to ask, she would have told them it was too painful to be near the caskets, even if it meant being near her family. She had to be alone with her thoughts, her grief.

She smoothed a long strand of auburn hair back beneath her kapp. She'd been a little lax with her grooming that day, her mind a million miles away.

Just like Susan was. A million miles away, in Heaven. Of course she was in Heaven. That was the only place a person like her could go.

Gloria wiped another tear, one of many endlessly streaming down her face.

There was a bit of a commotion at the barn doors. Gloria turned to see who had entered, and was surprised to see an Englischer. His tan suit, brown shoes and sunglasses set him apart right away. So did his lack of facial hair, as all men his age in the Amish faith grew beards after baptism.

He looked around the room, removing the glasses in order to see better. In the light from the oil lamps hanging from the rafters, Gloria finally recognized him. He was some sort of a policeman. She had seen him over the last three days, here and there. Normally hanging around on the edges of crowds, looking and listening. It was unnerving, feeling as though she and her people were being observed like that. Unnerving but not unusual, since being watched by Englischers was a fact of life for the Amish. Whenever Gloria went to town to sell her quilts, there was never any shortage of Englischers watching and pointing, whispering behind their hands. They'd even pulled up to her family's home on many occasions in their cars. As though the Amish existed as a form of entertainment.

This man at least seemed respectful. He kept his distance from the group of mourners. He was only going his job, Gloria reminded herself. He wasn't watching out of curiosity. She did wish he would have picked a better time to visit, though.

She couldn't take her eyes from him, even though she knew she should. He was fascinating. And handsome. This was the first chance she'd had to observe him, instead of the other way around. His dark brown hair, the bit of shadow on his cheeks. He looked tired—Gloria thought he must have been spending endless hours on the case, and her heart went out to him. He was trying to find the person responsible for the tragedy which befell her family. It meant more than he knew, she was sure.

He caught the eye of her Daed, who touched his wife's arm to get her attention. She turned and, when she saw the officer, rose from her chair. Gloria stood immediately. It was one thing for a stranger, policeman or no, to be there. It was another for him to bother her mother in her time of grief.

By the time she reached them, he was already asking questions. She heard him say something about additional family members, but her mother shook her head. When she reached them, Gloria placed a concerned hand on her mother's shoulder and turned to face the officer.

His eyes fell on her. "Excuse me, miss, but I have some questions for your mother which I think would be best asked solely of her."

So he knew who she was already. He'd already been asking questions, evidently.

"I'm sure you do, and I would like to hear them for myself." She turned to her mother. "Is that all right?"

"If the detective does not mind."

Gloria turned to the detective and waited with an expectant smile. He must have known there was no way for him to dissuade her, though it was obvious from the way he cleared his throat before speaking that he wasn't over-fond of speaking in front of her.

"Actually, I don't have anything else to ask. I wanted to assure you that we're doing everything in our power to find the culprit behind the crime." He smiled at Gloria. "We've never actually met. I'm Detective Paul Miller."

"Gloria Kauffman," she replied, smiling slightly.

"I'm very sorry for your loss, Miss Kauffman." He smiled at her Mamm and shook her hand. The smile changed his face—he was normally so serious, stern. When he smiled he looked younger. "I'll leave you, now. I'm sorry to have disrupted the wake."

"Would you like to stay for refreshments?" Gloria smiled fondly at her Mamm, who was cordial and kind even in the worst of times.

"No, thank you, ma'am. I'm sure you would rather proceed without the reminder of the police hanging around. Thank you for the offer." He nodded at the two of them and left the barn.

Gloria couldn't stand to see him go without finding out more. She ran after him, not caring who saw. Finding out about the arson was more important.

"Excuse me," she murmured when she caught up to him. She touched him arm purely out of reflex, then pulled her hand back as though he burned to the touch.

He turned back to her. "Yes, Miss Kauffman?"

"Detective, is there any new information about the murderer? Anything at all?"

He frowned. "Miss Kauffman, it's very unusual for a detective to discuss a case with the family of the victim before there's any sure suspect. I can't share speculation with you."

Her frown mirrored his. "But you do know something?"

"I can't tell you either way. I'm sorry, I'm sure it's frustrating. We're just as frustrated at the station, believe me." He turned away as if to go, and she touched his arm again. Again, she felt it was improper, but she was desperate.

"Miss Kauffman, it would be best if you go back in with your family. You need each other at a time like this. Let us do our job, and we'll let you know if there's any further news. You'll be the first to know, in fact." Again, he turned away.

Gloria went around him, standing in his way. He sighed in exasperation.

"I want to help you."

His eyes went wide. They were a deep blue, the color of the sky at twilight. "You what?"

"I want to help. I'm sure there's something I can tell you that you don't already know."

"You mean there are secrets we aren't aware of?"

She blushed and took a step back. "No. I didn't mean it that way."

"How did you mean it, then?"

"I only meant to say that I'm close with the family. Susan was like my sister. We Amish—we're close, anyway. We live our lives together, helping one another. We depend on each other. I'm sure you don't know that."

"I'm sure I don't," he said, with a wry smile.

"So you see, we know a lot about each other. Add to that my closeness with my cousin and, well, you see what I mean. I'm sure I can offer something of value to the investigation."

He looked skeptical, his eyes narrowing. "I'm not sure. We already know a lot about the family. We've spoken to the neighbors, for miles in all directions."

"I grew up with them. I'm sure there's something you've missed. I only want the chance to help."

She felt his eyes on her as he sized her up, and drew herself up to her full height. She was small, especially when compared to his tall height, but she was stronger than she looked. The detective would find that out, if he ever gave her a chance.

"You won't leave me alone until I agree to talk with you, will you?" His face wore a wry smile. He had a dry sense of humor, Gloria noticed.

She had to smile, too. "No, I won't. You'll be saving yourself a lot of time if you just let me have my say. I know you won't regret it."

He shrugged. "All right. What if we meet at the coffee shop tomorrow afternoon?"

The smile faded from her face. "The funeral is tomorrow afternoon."

"Oh. That was clumsy of me."

Gloria swallowed over the lump in her throat. "That's all right. You didn't mean it."

"I plan to be at the funeral as well—standing off to the back, of course. I wouldn't want to get in the way."

This surprised her so much, she forgot the threat of tears. "Why would you do that?"

"It's something we do—the police, I mean. I want to be there to keep an eye out for any suspicious looking people."

"But only the Amish will be there. People like me. You don't think it was someone from the community, do you?"

He winced. "No. And I think that should be as much as we discuss about it. I'll meet up with you after the services are finished."

Gloria's eyes cut toward the barn. She wondered how her family would feel about her running off to meet with an Englischer, detective or not. It was all in the name of getting answers, though.

"All right. I'll look for you."

"I don't think it'll be too tough to find me." He grinned, and Gloria giggled before she could help herself. Yes, he would stand out in his fine suit, so unlike the plain clothes of her people.

She hurried back to the barn, then, fearful of being discovered with the Englischer. Giggling when everyone else was in mourning. The talk would never end.

The Amish Detective: The King Family Arsonist

Made in the USA
Middletown, DE
28 May 2020

96225003R00049